BILLY GOATS GRUFF
AND OTHER STORIES

RETOLD BY SUSAN PRICE
ILLUSTRATED BY MOIRA & COLIN MACLEAN

Kingfisher Books, Grisewood & Dempsey Ltd,
Elsley House, 24–30 Great Titchfield Street, London W1P 7AD

First published in 1992 by Kingfisher Books.
2 4 6 8 10 9 7 5 3 1

The material in this edition was previously published by Kingfisher Books in
The Kingfisher Treasury of Nursery Stories (1990).

Text © Susan Price 1990, 1992
Illustrations © Colin and Moira Maclean 1990, 1992

BRITISH LIBRARY CATALOGUING IN PUBLICATION DATA
A catalogue record for this book is available from the British Library

ISBN 0 86272 893 2

Printed and bound in Spain

CONTENTS

◆ BILLY GOATS GRUFF ◆

Once upon a time, there were three billy goats: Little Billy Goat Gruff, Middle-Sized Billy Goat Gruff and Great Big Billy Goat Gruff. They'd had nothing to eat all winter but hay, so in the spring they set off for the mountain meadows, to eat the sweet, new, juicy, spring grass.

"You two go ahead," said Great Big Billy Goat Gruff. "There's a thistle or two here I mean to eat before I go on." So Middle-Sized Billy Goat Gruff and Little Billy Goat Gruff went on without him.

Then, "You go on ahead," said Middle-Sized Billy Goat Gruff to Little Billy Goat Gruff. "There's just one or two leaves on this thorn-bush I mean to eat before I go on." So Little Billy Goat Gruff went on alone.

To reach the mountain meadow where the sweet, new, juicy, spring grass grew, Little Billy Goat Gruff had to cross a wooden bridge over a high waterfall. Under the bridge lived a troll; a horrible, howling, gobbling, greedy troll. As Little Billy Goat Gruff crossed the bridge, his hooves went trip-trip-trip on the wooden planks. The troll underneath heard, and yelled out, "Who's trip-tripping across my bridge?"

"It's only me," said Little Billy Goat Gruff. "I'm just going to get fat on the sweet, new, juicy, spring grass over there in the meadow."

The troll was furious. He jumped up onto the bridge in front of Little Billy Goat Gruff. "Nobody crosses *my* bridge!" he yelled. "I'm going to eat you, little goat. I'm going to eat you from your horns to your heels."

"Oh, please don't eat me, you wouldn't enjoy me!" said Little Billy Goat Gruff. "I'm so small and skinny, I'd hardly be a mouthful. Wait for my brother, Middle-Sized Billy Goat Gruff. He'd make a much better meal."

The troll thought about it. "You *are* skinny," he said. "Hardly worth chewing. Yes, get off my bridge! I'll wait for your brother."

Little Billy Goat Gruff ran quickly across the bridge, trip-trip-trip, and was soon among the sweet, new, juicy,

spring grass on the other side, eating as much as he could. The troll went back under the bridge and waited.

Soon Middle-Sized Billy Goat Gruff had finished the leaves on the thorn-bush and came across the bridge. His middle-sized hooves went trot-trot-trot on the wooden planks. The troll underneath heard, and yelled out, "Who's trot-trotting across my bridge?"

"Only me," said Middle-Sized Billy Goat Gruff. "I'm going to the meadow, to eat the sweet, new, juicy, spring grass."

Up onto the bridge jumped the troll. He was furious. "Nobody crosses *my* bridge," he screamed. "I'm going to eat you, every scrap of you, from your horns to your heels. That'll teach you to trot-trot your nasty hooves across *my* bridge."

"You don't want to eat me," said Middle-Sized Billy Goat Gruff. "I'm not nearly big enough to fill your belly."

"You're bigger than your skinny little brother," said the troll.

"Yes," said Middle-Sized Billy Goat Gruff, "but I'm not nearly as big as our brother, Great Big Billy Goat Gruff. He's twice as big as me. Now *he* would make a meal fit for a troll."

The troll thought about it. "You're right," he said. "It makes sense to wait for the biggest of you. Get off my bridge then, before I eat you anyway!"

Middle-Sized Billy Goat Gruff ran quickly across the bridge and reached the meadow where Little Billy Goat Gruff was eating the sweet, new, juicy, spring grass.

Soon Great Big Billy Goat Gruff had finished his thistles, so he started across the wooden bridge to join his brothers. Tramp, tramp, tramp went his great big hooves on the wooden planks. Underneath the troll was listening and roared, "Who's tramp-tramping across my bridge?"

"I am," said Great Big Billy Goat Gruff. "I'm going to join my brothers

in the meadow and we're all going to
get fat."

The troll was furious to hear that. He
jumped up onto the bridge and landed in
front of Great Big Billy Goat Gruff.
"Nobody crosses *my* bridge!" said the troll.

"I'm crossing it," said Great Big Billy
Goat Gruff.

"No you're not!" screamed the troll. "I'm
going to eat you up, horns, hair and heels —
you're going to fill my belly until it feels as
if I've eaten half the world. I'm going to — "

"Come and try!" said Great Big Billy
Goat Gruff. He lowered his big-horned
head and said:

"On my head are two sharp spears;
With them I'll make you cry salt tears!
On my head are two big stones:
I'll thump you hard and smash your bones!"
Then he charged at the troll and speared
him, thumped him and tossed him right
over the sun and moon. High in the air
soared the troll, then down, down, down
he fell.

But he didn't land on the bridge —
he missed the bridge altogether and fell
even farther, down, down, down the
waterfall until SPLASH! that was
the end of the troll.

Great Big Billy Goat Gruff crossed the bridge, tramp, tramp, tramp, and joined his brothers in the meadow on the other side. They all got fat eating the sweet, new, juicy, spring grass. For all I know, they're still there, growing fatter and fatter every day.

And that's all I know of them, because snip, snap, snout, this tale's told out.

BRER RABBIT
◆ AND THE TAR-BABY ◆

Foxes like eating rabbits, and Brer Fox had been trying, for a long time, to catch Brer Rabbit and eat him. But Brer Rabbit always managed to get away somehow, by one trick or another. It made Brer Fox mad.

Now Brer Fox was walking along the road one day, and he came across some tar that had been left there. It was a hot day, and the tar was soft and sticky in the sun. Brer Fox thought of a way he could use that sticky tar to catch Brer Rabbit.

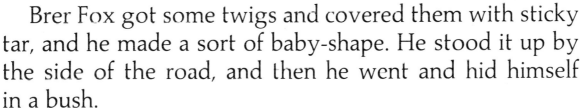

Brer Fox got some twigs and covered them with sticky tar, and he made a sort of baby-shape. He stood it up by the side of the road, and then he went and hid himself in a bush.

"You stand there, sticky tar-baby," said Brer Fox. "You wait for Brer Rabbit. He gets away from me, but he won't get away from you!"

After a while, along came Brer Rabbit, hopping and jumping with his tail stuck up behind him.

Brer Rabbit saw the tar-baby standing by the side of the road, and he called out, "Good morning to you!"

The tar-baby said nothing.

Well, Brer Rabbit thought the tar-baby hadn't heard him, so he went a bit closer and he spoke a bit louder.

"Good morning!" he said. "It's a fine day."

The tar-baby said nothing.

"Are you deaf?" shouted Brer Rabbit. "I said 'Good morning' to you twice, and you just stand there saying nothing. Some folk would think that rude."

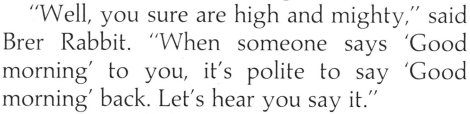

The tar-baby said nothing.

"Well, you sure are high and mighty," said Brer Rabbit. "When someone says 'Good morning' to you, it's polite to say 'Good morning' back. Let's hear you say it."

But the tar-baby said nothing.

Brer Rabbit was angry. "If you don't say 'Good morning', I'm going to let you have one right on the chin!"

The tar-baby still said nothing.

So Brer Rabbit punched the tar-baby right on the chin. But the tar-baby was sticky, and

Brer Rabbit's paw stuck to the tar.
No matter how Brer Rabbit pulled,
he couldn't get his paw free.

"Let me go!" Brer Rabbit shouted,
while Brer Fox laughed to himself in
the bush nearby. "Let me go or I'll
hit you with the other paw!"
But the tar-baby said nothing and
didn't let Brer Rabbit go.
So Brer Rabbit hit the tar-baby as hard
as he could with the other paw. And his
other paw got stuck too. Now Brer Rabbit
had both front paws stuck to the tar-baby,
and he couldn't get loose, no matter how he
struggled. "Let me go," said Brer Rabbit,
"or I'll kick you!"
But the tar-baby didn't let him go.
So Brer Rabbit kicked the tar-baby, and
got his foot stuck in the sticky tar, and couldn't
get it loose. Then Brer Rabbit kicked the tar-
baby with the other foot, and that got stuck
too. So there was Brer Rabbit, with all four feet
stuck in the tar, and he couldn't get loose, no
matter how he struggled and yelled.
Then Brer Fox came out of his bush, laughing.

"You think you're so clever," said Brer Fox, "but you're just a plain fool. I'm going to eat you, Brer Rabbit, and that'll be the end of you!"

"Oh," said Brer Rabbit, "cook me and eat me and I hope you enjoy me. That's not half as bad as what I thought you were going to do."

Brer Fox was puzzled.

"What did you think I was going to do?" he asked.

"Oh, I thought you were going to throw me in the briar patch."

"Throwing you in the briar patch is worse than cooking and eating you?"

"Oh, yes!"

"Well then, I'll hang you from a tree," said Brer Fox. "That'll be worse than eating you."

"Hang me from a tree, cook me and eat me," said Brer Rabbit, "only please, please don't throw me in a briar patch!"

"Then I *will* throw you in the briar patch!" said Brer Fox, and he tore Brer Rabbit off the tar-baby and threw him right into the middle of the briar patch. "There!" shouted Brer Fox. "Serves you right, Brer Rabbit!"

But not a sound came from Brer Rabbit in the briar patch. Brer Fox stopped and listened. Then he heard singing — Brer Rabbit *singing* in the briar patch!

This is the song:

"I was born and bred in a briar patch, Brer Fox!
Thorns'll never hurt me, Brer Fox!
I've lived all my life in a briar patch, Brer Fox!
I'm right where I want to be, Brer Fox!"

So Brer Rabbit tricked Brer Fox and got away, again! Brer Fox sneaked off and didn't dare show his face for a good many days. All the rabbits would have laughed at him if he had.

And that's the end of the story — but it was a good one while it lasted.

◆ THE GINGERBREAD MAN ◆

Once upon a time, there was an old woman who was baking. She made a gingerbread man for tea. She cut him out of spicy gingerbread and gave him currants for his eyes and mouth and currant buttons down his front. Then she put him in the oven to bake.

A little while later, there was a knock at the door. Not the kitchen door – the oven door! A voice shouted, "Let me out! Let me out!"

So the old woman opened the oven door and *whoosh!* the gingerbread man raced past her, across the kitchen floor and out into the garden. The old woman ran after him, shouting, "Come back! I baked you for tea!"

But the gingerbread man only laughed and ran on, calling, "Run, run, as fast as you can – you won't catch me, I'm the gingerbread man!"

The old woman's husband was digging in the garden, and he blinked when he saw the gingerbread man run past. Then he saw his wife running after him and heard her

16

shouting, "Stop that gingerbread man! He's for our tea!"
So the old man dropped his spade and ran after the
gingerbread man too.

"Stop!" he shouted. "You're for our tea!"

But the gingerbread man only laughed. "Your wife
can't catch me and nor will you! Run, run, as fast as you can
— you'll never catch me, I'm the gingerbread man!"

And he ran on, down the road, with the old man and the
old woman panting after him.

He ran past a cow, and the cow smelled the spicy
gingerbread. "Mmm!" said the cow. "Come back, I want to
eat you."

But the gingerbread man only laughed. "The old
woman can't catch me, nor the old man. And no cow in the
world can! Run, run, as fast as you can — you won't catch
me, I'm the gingerbread man!"

And on he ran. The cow came lumbering after him, and panting along behind the cow came the old man and the old woman, all three of them chasing the runaway gingerbread man.

The gingerbread man ran past a horse, and the horse smelled the spicy gingerbread. "Hey!" said the horse. "Come back! I'd like to eat you!"

But the gingerbread man only laughed. "The old woman can't catch me, nor the old man; the cow can't catch me, and no horse in the world can! Run, run, as fast as you can – you won't catch me, I'm the gingerbread man!"

And on he ran. After him the horse came galloping, and behind the horse the cow came lumbering, and panting along behind the cow came the old man and the old woman, all chasing the runaway gingerbread man.

Then the gingerbread man ran past some haymakers who were working in a field. The haymakers smelled the spicy gingerbread and said:

"Ooh! Come back, gingerbread man! We'd like to eat you!"

But the gingerbread man only laughed and said:

"The old woman can't catch me, nor the old man; the cow can't, the horse can't and no one in the world can. So run, run, as fast as you can — you won't catch me, I'm the gingerbread man!"

And on he ran; and after him ran all the haymakers, shouting; and behind them came the horse, galloping; and behind them, the cow, lumbering; and behind them, the old man and the old woman, panting. All of them chasing the runaway gingerbread man.

But ahead of the gingerbread man was a wide, deep river. By the edge of the river sat a fox, watching everything.

The gingerbread man had to stop when he reached the river. He couldn't go into the water, or he would melt.

"Now what are you going to do?" asked the fox.

The gingerbread man was afraid of the fox, but he still said:

"Run run as fast as you can — you won't catch me, I'm the gingerbread man!"

"I don't want to run," said the fox, "and I don't want to catch you. I never eat gingerbread — it's bad for my teeth. Would you like me to carry you across the river?"

"You won't eat me?" asked the gingerbread man.

"You can sit on my tail, which is farthest from my mouth. I can't eat you then, can I?" said the clever fox.

The gingerbread man got onto the fox's tail and the fox started to swim across. The haymakers, the horse, the cow, the old man and the old woman all ran down to the river bank, too late. The gingerbread man waved to them from the fox's tail and shouted, "Run, run, as fast as you can — you won't catch me, I'm the gingerbread man!"

As the fox swam across the river, his tail got wet, so the gingerbread man climbed a little farther up to the fox's back.

As the fox swam on, the river got deeper, and more and

more of his back was under water. The gingerbread man
had to move up farther, onto the fox's shoulders. But soon
even the fox's shoulders were wet.

"Climb onto my head," said the fox. "You'll be dry
there."

So the gingerbread man climbed up onto the fox's head.
But soon even the fox's head got splashed. Only his nose
was poking above the surface.

"Climb onto my nose," said the fox. "You'll be dry
there."

So the gingerbread man climbed onto the fox's nose.
Just as the fox reached the other side of the river, and was

climbing out onto the bank, he gave his nose a quick *flip!* Up into the air sailed the gingerbread man. The fox opened his mouth wide. Down fell the gingerbread man, right into the fox's mouth – SNAP!

The fox sat on the bank and looked at the haymakers, the horse, the cow, the old man and the old woman on the other side. He licked his lips and said, "Run, run, as fast as you can – it takes a fox to catch a gingerbread man!"

Because foxes are clever, and they know that it takes more to catch gingerbread men than running after them shouting, "Come back! I want to eat you!"